THE DOG'S COLLAR

A ZACH A. QUINN MYSTERY

AF582133

REYHAN HAPPY

Copyright © Reyhan Happy
All Rights Reserved.

This book has been self-published with all reasonable efforts taken to make the material error-free by the author. No part of this book shall be used, reproduced in any manner whatsoever without written permission from the author, except in the case of brief quotations embodied in critical articles and reviews.

The Author of this book is solely responsible and liable for its content including but not limited to the views, representations, descriptions, statements, information, opinions and references ["Content"]. The Content of this book shall not constitute or be construed or deemed to reflect the opinion or expression of the Publisher or Editor. Neither the Publisher nor Editor endorse or approve the Content of this book or guarantee the reliability, accuracy or completeness of the Content published herein and do not make any representations or warranties of any kind, express or implied, including but not limited to the implied warranties of merchantability, fitness for a particular purpose. The Publisher and Editor shall not be liable whatsoever for any errors, omissions, whether such errors or omissions result from negligence, accident, or any other cause or claims for loss or damages of any kind, including without limitation, indirect or consequential loss or damage arising out of use, inability to use, or about the reliability, accuracy or sufficiency of the information contained in this book.

Made with ♥ on the Notion Press Platform
www.notionpress.com

To,

My friends and family,

For always supporting me and being my net whenever I fell back!

And, to my school,

For giving me the power of learning the English Language and use it as a tool for expressing my purpose; and for helping me get to this book.

This book is what I'm giving back. My first "Opening Ticket".

Contents

Preface *vii*

Acknowledgements *ix*

Foreword *xiii*

Prologue *xvii*

1. A "Wonderful" Letter To The Principal 1

2. An "Encounter" With My AEF 5

3. A "Bone Breaking" Bus Trip 9

4. An "Eventful" Covert Opp 13

5. An "Intro" To School/ And My "Shaky"Apology 17

6. A "Hint & Command" 21

7. A "Second "Riddle & "Encounter" With Edd 23

8. A "Prelude" To The Dog's Collar 26

9. A "Stolen" Dark Gem 30

10. A "Clash" With The "Three Musketeers" 33

11. A "Bull-y Chase" 37

12. A "Hero" Who Wore The "Fireball 2879" 40

13. Conclusion 44

Preface

When I started writing the book, I didn't think I would be able to finish writing the story or its draft 1. I started writing the story approximately three years ago, and I thought I would finish it within 9 months. I finished it in 2 and a half years. Not only that, but I wanted my story to be something everyone could connect to (around the age of 6 - 16) and I wanted everyone to know they could also write stories (and maybe make a change in the world in that way). As hardly any books are made by children for children, to connect with the way they think or how they feel when they are in their school years. So I wanted to write a story about a character in my mind I used to play with, who can connect with you or the younger you (if you are an adult). Now I am not saying everything is going to connect with you but enjoy the story along the way. This character I've made is fictional, and he has a mix of talents everyone has, but he has found his problem-solving passion. While writing this book, I felt many emotions and mental blocks in how I wrote the story. I had also felt that my story was not good enough, but I came around it. This character is one of my favourite things about the story; The setting and plot all came with the character. He is my imaginary friend (The one who I talk to in my mind when I'm alone) so I thought why not make him the character of my story, then it took a huge turn after I started writing the story.

Acknowledgements

I am forever and ever indebted to all the help(space, kindness) provided by my dear Editors/ Facilitators Poorva Ma‘am and Sreeja Ma’am; to Mom and Dad for giving me unconditional love, support and experience throughout the journey (And when I sat at the table asking them to help me edit, though I hadn’t yet finished my homework.).

I am incredibly grateful for all the support I received from my Mom, Dad and great-grandmother who gave me ideas and help with sentence structure and literary devices.

I hope that my (facilitators/mentors) are happy seeing how I used all the English classes we’ve had (Especially the ones on story writing). I thank Poorva Ma‘am, Shruthy Ma’am, Sreeja Ma‘am, and Disha Ma’am, as well as, Nagendra sir and Umesh sir for unlimited free time in the school lab which supported me a lot in this process. I thank my dad/mentor/facilitator - Happy Sir for all his advice on using different perspectives and emotions for each of my characters.

I owe my peers gratitude as they supported me on this journey with questions and Ideas that helped my book get better. - to Ashraf and Manha for asking me questions about loopholes that were in my story, to Neha V. for being one of my peers who didn’t judge my story.

I love how I was influenced by fellow writers of my age who had started this journey along with me and helped me overcome writer’s block every time I felt I was failing. I hope I can make a difference in your confidence towards publishing your first book. Thank you Lakshita (who helped me with perspectives of different kinds of stereotypical people), Adwaith (my best friend), Aashna (my fellow literature buddy), Pritesh (who helped me visualize twists for my book with descriptions from my favourite anime), Archita (who told me in dramatic and lyrical ways my book had flaws), Mrityunjay (my friend who started writing along with me) I hope you guys publish your books as well.

So much love to my four seniors in my school for being my inspirations and my big sisters/brothers when I boasted about my book to my friends. So much love to Mihika, Aaryan Samriddhi and Simran. Thank you for reading the first draft of my book to assure me that children will like it. Thanks again Simran for giving me ideas on how to illustrate my book.

Thank You so much Writers/Creators who I looked up to when I was young helped me get such imaginative powers. thank you for being my Idols - Enid Blyton, Roald Dahl, Ruskin Bond, Sarah J. Maas, Cassandra Clare, Rick Riordan, J.R.R. Tolkien, Sudha Murthy and my beloved creators Michael Jackson who asked me if *I was okay (Annie, Are you okay? Are you okay? Are you okay? Are you okay, Annie?)* and Stan Lee and the MCU for being such amazing creators.

Thank you all!!! For how much you've given this world, as this is what I'm giving back. I'm also happy that I can return to the world something, after all, it gave me the power of English and Writing.

I would really love to know how you liked this book if you read it, as I think it would help my future ones as well. I also really appreciate the support you have given me by buying this book of mine and hence if you think you have feedback for me (specific places you liked about the book, and specific places you didn't) E-mail it to me at reyhanhappyofficial@gmail.com, for me to implement the feedback and use it in my next book.

With Love,
Reyhan Happy

Foreword

In my work as a writer and as an educator, I have come across tons of people who wish to write a book (safe to say, everyone has dreamt about writing a book at some point in their lives, or will dream about it!).

However, what it takes to make this dream a reality - is something most people do not talk about or always go through. It takes courage - to see your idea - in all its raw reality in front of you - ready to be judged, interpreted and morphed. It then takes more courage to actually morph that idea into the idea that you want it to be!

And morphing ideas, ideas that exist in transient, sublime forms in your consciousness, into tangible words, paragraphs and plotlines - is an act of courage and immense resilience.

The author of this book, whom I have known and mentored since he was 10 years old, has worked on this courage and resilience - from not wanting to express his ideas on paper lest they become real to expressing them and then not being able to muster the courage to look at them again to working through drafts and drafts and drafts. He has grappled with content-level edits, structural edits, syntactical edits (unlearning and learning grammar concepts in the process!); and seen this work of fiction through seemingly unending tunnels to the light of the page!

Anyone who has written a book or tried to write a book (including myself!) knows what a remarkable feat that is!

What you are about to read, then, is an actualization of his act of courage. And I have always believed that in the act of creation of any writing - what we really transfer to the reader (or listener) is the emotion we put into it. Given that, I wish that every reader of this book is filled with the courage to put their ideas, thoughts and desires into tangible forms - the courage to make one's voice heard and seen in tangible forms.

Now, 'voice' is something quite complex. How does one find one's voice and then express it in one's writing? The 6+1 traits of writing (which Reyhan has learned to incorporate into this book) has Voice as one of the traits. Voice is the unique style and personality of the writing that is particular to the author. Many times, there is a foreclosure we experience as writers, wherein we may imitate or be too influenced by authors we have read or what we think our 'voice' SHOULD sound like.

Developing one's own voice in writing is as complex and important a task as developing one's own voice in life! It involves thinking deeply about each choice we make. And Reyhan, in the writing process, has tried very hard to find, develop, shape and bring forth his 'voice' as a child growing up in a particular school and community in this current interconnected world. By bringing forth this voice - he is really trying to say something more - which is beyond the plot and twists of the story.

I do hope that it is this 'voice' that reaches you all as you read this book. For, this voice that he wants to put forth is a vision to connect with many other voices of children like him. And he felt like this voice needed to be heard. I agree!

As a children's book author and language educator - I have felt that a lot of work in children's fiction has the voice of adults. Sometimes, good literature has the voice of adults that really sees children and tries to see or know the world through their eyes. It is still not a child's voice.

Therefore, I think this is an important work of fiction - which is in the voice of a child with the aim to reach and amplify more voices of children.

Do not confuse the voice of the child to be the same as a 'childish' voice! Not for one bit! Not at all! The writer of this book has keenly seen the world around him and his friends, reflected on it and wants to present it in all its glory, mystery and complexity.

Finally, it is my hope that every reader of this book will be able to relate to the idea of mystery and how we deal with it, find clues and evolve to solve it; to the dynamics that shape our friendships and peer relationships and to the humour that we find in it all!

Lastly, to everyone who reads this book - please do send in your comments and feedback to the author, as that will be invaluable to his growth to the author in developing his 'voice' which will reflect back to you in his future writing.

With great joy and excitement, I invite you to accompany the fastidious Zach A. Quinn and his eclectic group of friends on solving their very first mystery!

Like Reyhan, I hope you all find your words to say what you want to say -

Love and Light,

Poorva Agarwal

(Author and Facilitator)

Prologue

My name is Zach Quinn, and I'm a pretty cool kid. I love video games and football. "Ice cream, I hear. And I'm there. I have friends. I go to a (not-so-normal school), and I love vampires, werewolves, and comic stuff. And I am kind of a nobody in school, but something people don't know is that I'm a Spy(fine, I admit some people know it. The hall monitors, the principal, all the secret agents/Spies, and my archenemy) which is a part of my job, in this school. Try guessing which grade I am in

(4 cm smile)

(162 cm tall)

(24 cm wide)

(Straight back)

(Dark blue eyes)

(Thick dark Brown hair)

(2.1 cm long nose)

(1.8 cm wide eyes)

|

|

|

|

|

Yup, a 6th grader!

Thursday. Morning, 8:45 AM After Gym class

Have you ever run away from a bully? My full-time job (that is).

Through the corner of my eyes. I saw that I was cornering myself. But they seemed to be looking away from me, But, to the principal. He sits on the other side of the cafeteria (in the ' VIP cabin' that looks like a demolished part of a place close to the violent Mount Etna), (a terrifying volcano in Europe). People were gawking at me with the queerest looks.

Only because the Bully had duct tape in his hand. (to stick me to the wall, of course.) I felt like I was getting the type of attention that you get when people feel sorry for you, the one sort of attention I hate getting.

"Man, why couldn't I have just let them do what they wanted!" I muttered under my breath. And my brain screamed back at me. "Because we do what is right. Now stop being such a crybaby, get to the principal with your information, and let him handle the rest!"

Maybe I should fill you in on an unerring tale about me.

ONE

A "Wonderful" Letter to the Principal

Sunday. 5 PM, Principal's House.

Everything started a week ago. I had been hunting for the principal's house (with my buddies) down the street from mine. The lane where the principal lived, was known as the "Rich Neighbourhood" since it housed a variety of wealthy and famous people. I genuinely think the people were just rich to be rich because I haven't seen them do anything lavish for their neighbourhood, or even try to throw a party. In reality, I've seen waterless pools and freshly asphalt roads damaged because of their ideologies on how things should be.

I'd biked about our township a lot since moving here, and I'd never been exposed to this neighbourhood before. The alley has been in use for at least 30 years. It used to be on a tiny slope that led into a quarry. However, that was demolished and then utilised for industrialisation after the government discovered that they were engaging in illegal activities (don't ask me what they discovered, because we moved to this flat two years ago and I haven't heard anything from the aunties in the neighbourhood).

Coming back to the point, we wanted to talk to him about a school issue.

But to our fateful surprise, he'd got egged on (His house, I mean). It was a must-watch - him cleaning his house. He had to clean it down and repaint it he said. We moved closer to him, but not too close, and then he gave us a disdainful look. I got the impression he thought we were the ones who egged his house, but then he said,

"Don't tell anyone about what happened. It occurs at least once a month. It's not a problem for me."

"But, how is it that in such a highly protected and valuable neighbourhood such feats can be achieved?" I asked

"It's called a "wretched neighbourhood" for a reason looks like" Jayden mumbled

We nodded and approached him with our concerns. I wrote it in my finest handwriting and gave it to him. We all stepped back from him so that no paint would get on our clothes. He read aloud the letter.

Dear Principal Tom,

This letter conveys some happenings in school that needs to be addressed quickly.

I had gone to the rooftop following a boy yesterday. The boy had a bulging bag that looked very suspicious, as you are supposed to leave your things in the locker before you shift to another class.

When I opened the door to the platform on the rooftop, there were dozens of students selling anything ranging from toys to candies. If we don't shut this up, the whole school won't have children in classes, but the rooftop.

I hope you understand. Here below is a small video our group took about getting the kids to do this...

From Zach, Jake, Jayden, Kelly, and Faren.

"How come you didn't tell me about this sooner?" "I could've helped, seriously," said Principal Tom. "I could've come up with a solution and talked to the person in charge of these things."

"That's why we decided to embark on a clandestine operation to catch these men." "It's no fun just talking to them," Jake explained.

"Practically, it would be a lot better than just sitting idle doing nothing." "It will not taste nice. We are clandestine operatives (know as "The Black Crystal") manifesting action, but there has been no action." "You know, it gets boring," Jayden stated.

"OK, then I'll go inside and watch the video." Make an effort not to disgrace yourself in front of the entire school, but make sure you bring the "Man held responsible" to me." Rolling his eyes, Principal Tom declared. "Aye, aye, Captain!" We all barked and walked away.

TWO

AN "ENCOUNTER" WITH MY AEF

Monday, 10:45 a.m.

"Is there ever a time when I don't hear my phone buzzing?" Jayden stated

"Huh, it's quite fun... you know," Jake answered with a shrug. "I'm missing class to complete an important mission."

"Anyway, why didn't you say what the problem was?" Jake said

"Then it won't be thrilling," I mimic his favourite video game character.

"Do you know where Faren is?" Jayden inquires, "I haven't seen her in a long time,"

"She is ill," I stated making the end of that.

Jake, Jayden, Kelly, and I made our way to the ER (Emergency Room). We began to hear strange sounds coming from the chamber, such as footsteps and youngsters whispering.

"I don't wanna go in there," Jayden said.

"Neither do I," Kelly said.

"Kay then, I still want to check it out," Jake exclaimed, excitedly.

We took our time approaching the door, making sure no one could hear us coming.

That's when I realised something was wrong. There were four pairs of shoes outside the room. They were kept nicely and appeared to be polished daily. They were large, so I assumed they belonged to our teachers. They were all the same size. So I assumed that the school shoe sponsors had provided them with those.

I was ready to turn towards Jake and tell him what I saw when I saw he wasn't there.

That's when something hit me so hard that I blacked out.

BANG!!!

I looked around twice before ending the assignment. I'm not sure what happened, but I know it was a long time.

After an indeterminate amount of time.

The first thought that sprang to me when I awoke was,

Is This Heaven........

Then someone said something.

"Hi, old friend," said the mysterious individual

I knew the moment I heard his voice. Fariq. Fariq Bates, my opposition, my archenemy, the kryptonite to my Superman, the water to my fire, the not friend, not ally, not spy, my..., that's right, My AEF (Arch/Enemy/Forever)

Getting sucked back to life, yet again. Right, I'm in front of this unlikable, disgusting, and short child of years 14 (he does not live up to his age).

"Do you remember me?" said the he.

"No, I don't think so. You hit me so hard that I forgot who you were, but if you turn on the lights, I might remember," I replied.

"Cut the drama"

"You cut it"

"You were the one who started it"

And he turned on the light.

"I need something from you right now." That's why I summoned you here," Fariq Bates said. My AEF.

"Of course you did! I had realised that even before you knocked me out cold,

"You could have asked nicely, but you just love using brute force," I said.

"Stop talking! "Please, allow me to speak," he said.

"Say that to yourself," I spoke back, disgusted.

He didn't say anything to me. So I went on.

"Anyway, why did you call me_?" But I was cut off as a cage fell around me.

"Come on!" I grunted as I tried to bang against the cage's closed door, but it wouldn't budge.

(I'm still in the cage, and we're still bickering) 15 minutes later

"Can I ask you a question?" I inquired of Fariq.

"Yes, what is it?" Fariq stated.

"What did you need me for?"

"Uh, well...Because I wanted you to get me the...," he explained. "the dogs collar, however

I got my 'bullies' to go take it instead."

"Wait, isn't that some sort of rumour or something?" I inquired.

"No, it's not. That's another reason I won't let you go: you'll try to stop my 'bullies'."

"Please let me go," I asked, "I want to go_"

"I simply stated NO!" He screams with a shrilly voice "All right?"

"No? "I'd like to return to class," I said.

"Please?" I request.

"N-O, No!" He responded,

"Please?" I say it again to irritate him.

"No!" He responds,

"Ple__" I almost say, but I'm cut off by a student council member who says...

"The principal would like to meet with you to discuss your feelings about the premium library membership." "And he'd like to come in here."

"Uhhh," He grunts, nodding with a smirk like he has something up his sleeve. Then he turns towards me. "Today is your lucky day, did you know?"

He presses a palm-sized red button in front of him, and the cage's side is opened. That manoeuvre astounded me. Who would suppose he was so considerate as to let me go? I get up and walk away from there, towards the exit.

"Thanks, I knew you'd make the right choice," I said, preparing to sprint if he sent someone after me. I was startled to learn that he let me off the hook.

I went to class, but it was the day's second to last lesson - I had missed my favourite subject, maths. I was hungry because I hadn't eaten anything during the snack and lunch breaks. After all, I had missed both of them.

After the last lesson, I went down to the lobby and packed my belongings for the trip home. When I noticed several of Fariq's bodyguards approaching, I rushed to the boy's washroom (YOU might call me a scaredy-cat for running away, but that's what I thought I should've done). I walked into the restroom and hid. I got out of there after 10 minutes and proceeded to the bus stop. Because of all the extra weight I was carrying (since I'd taken all the books in front of me from my locker when the bodyguards appeared and ran to hide in the boy's washroom), I took longer to get to my bus and hid behind my bus. When...

THREE

A "BONE BREAKING" BUS TRIP

Monday, 3 p.m.

I could hear the bell ring. I was so preoccupied with Fariq and his bodyguards that I assumed I was going on my bus, but I was mistaken. And then I realised my bus would be waiting for the preschoolers before leaving, so I had time. I put on my hoodie and rushed towards route 0422 (Jake's bus) and hid in a bush nearby, slowly but quickly approaching his window to ensure that after a brief conversation with him, I could escape to my bus before it realised I wasn't there.

It wasn't difficult for me to get to the window where he sat. The issue was that when my phone alarm began to ring "Tweep! Tweep! Tweep!" (Why didn't I put it on silent mode before going on the mission?) All the other kids on the bus stared at me. For some reason, the kindergarten students on the opposite bus began throwing water balloons, chocolate wrappers, paper planes, glue packets, Hair gel...?, paper rockets, blasting crackers, paper bombs, and other miscellaneous items at ME! Who knew they were stealing all of the kindergarten materials at the school (which is why Principal Tom asked if we knew where they were)? I suppose he now knows where it all went. Do you know how annoying it is when people throw random objects at you? To make matters worse, I noticed Jake sitting with someone who was wearing a cap and a scarf around his neck. He resembled.... "HUUUUUUUUHHHHHH............ My AEF with my BFF" (My AEF.) I exclaimed. To clarify, AEF stands for Arch/Enemy/Forever, similar to BFF)(and some kind of puzzle piece clicked in my brain) He betrayed me? That's how I found Fariq after I went unconscious. "What on earth does he think he's doing?" I grumbled angrily and muttered 'something' under my breath. Then something unexpected happened. My friend smiled as he glanced at me. Then a text message arrived with a "Tweep! Tweep! Tweep!" I rolled into Fariq and his bodyguards' blind spot just as Fariq and his bodyguards turned to gaze at the ground where I had been standing. Fortunately, I was on grass, or my footprints would have been visible. I was thankful that there were no glue sticks and hair gel this time to be thrown.

That's when the unseeable, unthinkable, undoable, 'thing' happens...

Have you ever gone underneath a bus and then the bus takes off, and you have no idea you're soaring through the air? Well, guess what, I didn't realise. Was it possible that the bus might start at any moment and my shoelace would become entangled in its wheels? I should listen to my mother and tie my shoelaces even if it only goes about 1 foot out of my shoes (thankfully, I learned my lesson). That's exactly what happened. My phone was about to ring again the moment I rolled to the side. I courageously turned down the ringtone volume because I had expected it. (I had to stretch my legs close to the back tyre of the bus to take out my headphones because I had permanently turned on the notification volume in my spy phone) and as the Tweep! Tweep! Tweep! Tweep! Tweep! Tweep! Tweep! Sound will entice the youngsters to come to me (much like how flies are drawn to the light in the dark). I was about to phone my parents and ask them to come to pick me up from school when the bus charged forward like a hyperactive child. And with that, I was gone.

Flying up and down, spinning around and around, my legs performing split jumping jacks, getting a few bruises on my arms and legs, and ultimately a thud that causes a streaking pain over my chest and complete quiet where I can't see or hear anything. The second unconsciousness of the day followed a minute or two later. What a great way to go!

Remind me to buy nicer shoes with shorter laces, because these shoes have such long laces I almost died.

One hour later

(However, I don't think Jake's bus driver noticed me doing unimaginable feats with my feet tied to the bus.) Instead, I awoke behind a supermarket, next to a dumpster. And I knew exactly where I was (the Pow Pow Ka-Pow store). Don't ask me who came up with that name). The store was approximately a kilometre from my house, and I went there every weekend. It was a gambit with free video games and candy.

I went into the store after finding my bag. I collected a few hundred candies and went out to buy the video game Jake and I were going to play this weekend (The Clash

Championship 2). Since I hadn't eaten, I paid my lunch money and some of the money I found in the dumpster to the clerk running the shop.

(Don't ask me if he smelled the money or anything) and dashed to my house. Whenever I go by bus I reach home at 5:45. Because my lane is the last stop, I time my run to end at 5:45.

Fortunately, the bus arrived when I did, giving the impression that I was dropped off. You may be asking if the driver checks on individuals who have been left behind. But I don't think he cares about who is left because no one assists him with Pick-ups and Drops. Hence, he drives like a robot from stop to stop. Our bus lacks teachers and support staff because the kindergarten bus needs them. (I wouldn't doubt it either; a glance at them transforms them into LITTLE DEVILS.) That is why OUR driver does not do anything other than follow his process.

I entered my house and shut the door. There was no one at home (I realised this because there was no sound). Then I headed down the hall. My mother was not preparing dinner. And my father wasn't working on his boat in the backyard.

That's when my ears exploded!

My friends had organised a party for my birthday!

(which I never seem to remember, my birthday, not the party)

So far, the day was going well. (Except for the two times I passed out) I suppose someone has to pay the price for a wonderful day.

Who would have guessed that my enraged pals would throw me a surprise birthday party? I suppose the day went nicely.

FOUR

An "Eventful" Covert Opp

Tuesday at 6:15 a.m.

So, I set my alarm clock for 6:00 a.m. yesterday. So I could cycle to school and the rooftop before any of those sugar monsters arrived. And conduct my own investigation.

I looked around to see whether there was anyone else in the school but myself, but I was astonished to find that just the principal and I were present. The principal was in his office, typing and reading as he always did. I entered the lift in the lobby and touched the button with the word R carved on it, which was carved on a small round teak wood that had become black since the school was established. It became black as a result of people going up there for no reason at all or for school functions because there is a stage on top, That can be transformed into a stage or a large timber structure with steel stands (it folds).

When I reached the roof, I hid on one of the lift's edges and peered out into the open space. Except for the sound of the generator and the staff's storage area, it was deserted. I crept backstage and slipped behind some equipment to get a better look at the room. I was astonished to see the door open, with intruders older than me. The voices, though, did not sound familiar.

"...and do we have the mind blast monocle for tomorrow? with the Ca_."

"Sir, we haven't gotten the _ thing from you yet, Boss."

"What time is the da_?"

I couldn't figure out why they weren't saying whole words, so I leaned forward to listen to them, but at that moment, a cello in front of me fell, causing a domino of uncontrollable instrument music (

(As in, a cello tipped over a violin, which tipped over a guitar, which tipped over a sitar, which tipped over a veena, which tipped a keyboard, which tipped a trumpet that fell inside a Grand Piano, when the trumpet fell there was an open water can next to it which was placed on the edge of a table and that fell too, and the water got equally distributed into the grand piano and onto the floor resulting in a choice pretty obvious.

RUN!!

I raced as fast as I could, but they were fast and on my heels. Then I took a sharp right and ran towards a rope on the far side of the structure. I sprang with all my power and stretched my arms out like a cheetah leaping towards a gazelle a dozen feet away. There is good news and not-so-good news and better news. First, I'll offer the good news. The good news was that I caught the rope; the not-so-good news was that it wasn't tied to anything but was jammed on a window in the science lab and fell loose when I caught ahold of it; and the better news was that I had my grapple hook in my pocket. I wish I could have told you I shot it to the principal's window, landed heroically, and then flipped on the ground... But that's not true since when I shot the hook, it flew out the open cafeteria window. Well, I believe when spies get their first tools/armoury, they test it out or something, and unhappily, I hadn't, as they said it 100% works and is easy to use, so there was no need to test. Now I couldn't figure out how to bring myself down. And I was two levels above ground. When all the school buses arrived, I attempted climbing up to the cafeteria as quickly as I could because my hand was slipping. Because the drivers park the buses adjacent to the building's sidewalls and we have a double-decker bus, I started moving back down so I could leap on top of the bus that would come and be under my feet at any second, now. And I jumped (by mistake forgetting what I was supposed to do) thinking I'd land on top, surprisingly, it swerved to the left and I was holding on to the side railings of the bus (as tight as I could) when the driver saw me in the rearview mirror and held the brake out of shock. I didn't anticipate him to stop, but I managed to use my feet and jump from the bus to a nearby tree, which turned out to be a bush formed into a tree.

I descended from the tree and dusted myself so that I could join my classmates in class before the bell rang. When I arrived only Jayden, Kelly, and Faren remained, and I understood why. I was about to strike up a conversation when Kelly stated

"Why didn't you take the bus, and why did you travel alone?"

"Yeah, why," Jayden answered, his face flushed with rage.

"I was going to say that," I explained.

But before I knew it, Kelly and Jayden had vanished.

"What? "

"They wanted an apology, not anything else," Faren explained.

"Oh" I let out a sigh.

"You are going to apologise, right?"

Everything in my head was telling me that I'm not the child who apologises, but the kid who doesn't. When a small itty bitty part of me said, "There is no I in spy team," (I guess there's a saying like that or something) and I made the right decision (the itty bitty ones', of course)

And marched with pride to my locker. I'm sure that was a lame way of saying it.

FIVE

An "Intro" to School/ And My "Shaky" Apology

Tuesday, on the way to BCHQ (Black Crystal Headquarters), 1:15 PM.

First and foremost, Yes, I apologised. I mean, I got a few grunts from Kelly, but Jayden listened and acknowledged, and we both fist-bumped, stating that we were fine, and I said I wouldn't go solo without alerting them. But Kelly accepted the apologies after a little empathy-receiving and then she ran away, a bit less hot-headed than before, which I would call an improvement. But I know she'll forget about it when I make Choco-cookie Ice Cream at home, or when she goes on another adventure, or when she forgets about it tomorrow. Yeah, I realise I care a little too much about her, but what can I do? She's my friend.

I was on my way to the Black Crystal Headquarters (BCHQ).

When the school was created, the principal believed it would be fun to form teams so that children could learn how to have varied interests and engage with other jobs they might obtain in life. So he formed the following teams:

1. The Spy Team - (where I am)
2. The Ball Team - Where they learn the art of balls, all games that involve balls.
3. The Samurai Team - The sickest/coolest/best team. They get to use swords and katanas and all different kinds of weapons.
4. The Pottery Team - They learn the art of how to use their hands, and survival techniques in the wild.
5. The Computer Team - They have the smartest people in school, and duh, the smartest of computers
6. The Ninja Team (good ninjas who aid, not bad ninjas who steal) - Just like The Samurai Team but they have a different discipline, a different style of fighting, and different mottos/aims
7. The Stunt Team - These guys learn the most dangerous techniques, that improve their flexibility, and strength, and lessen the number of fears they have. They are also one of the sickest teams as they learn parkour on the terrace of our school's second building.
8. The Agricultural Team - The most boring team, these guys have set out on a mission to plant 500 trees per year as they think the trees are going to help the problems in this world.

There was usually one commander who oversaw or assisted each team. Every time a new student arrived at school, he or she would find a note in their locker inviting them to join one of the teams (after they reviewed your resume or application)(There have been those who have not been picked) and they have the opportunity to make a decision. The cool thing about these teams is that they earn team tokens or team points, which you can cash in for school tokens to help your class or to buy snacks from the snack shack at the end of each term, and the team with the most points wins the life reality award, and somehow our team always comes in last. The person with the most points wins the Life Champion Award. Fariq and I tied for the award last year, but he cheated (as in food-poisoned me) and won, which is how he gained more favour and earned the award and got crowned president. (One of the reasons I dislike him). This year, our team will easily win more because we have a high point total, have upskilled ourselves, and have solved more than 50 cases. Our biggest case will be Fariq's case as he is the president and if he goes down all will be well, and we will have the award in the bag, and I will receive my well-deserved trophy.

The coolest part about it all is that each team enters a portal to reach their secret area. And nobody knows how to get into our room except the people on our squad. The way all of this gateway stuff works is... So you go to a desk in the research lab, press a button, and a microphone comes out, and then you say the password of your respective group, which allows you to open a portal that leads to your specific chamber.

This was created a year ago, and there was a new, extremely expensive technology that our principal had purchased, which is what some people use to get around. Even after all of this, most of these teams have spies who aid infiltrate and steal points, and if they are exposed, everything is gone. Except for our team, every other team is experiencing invasion and revealing. That's why our team received the **Dependable Team** award three times in a row, as well as the most **Action-Taking Team** once. This year, we will easily **annihilate** all of the other teams.

SIX

A "Hint & Command"

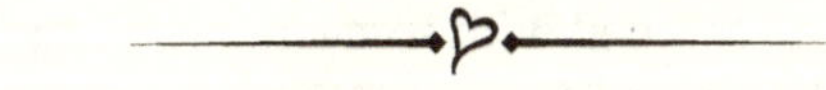

Tuesday, 1:30 p.m. at BCHQ.

When I arrived, the entire building was deserted; nobody was there, not even the higher-level BC personnel (those folks work non-stop for a week on only two meals a day). It was so quiet and silent that I could hear my footsteps echo in a rythmic beat. That's when I realised something was wrong.

I walked to my desk and opened my laptop and saw a message that said...

Hi,

I've captured your team as well as the higher level of BC. Do as I say to get them back.

Pick up a hint from the rubbish towards the back of the school and follow it.

Go to the west wing's nurse's station and pick up the Dog's collar

Do what I say, or big things will happen to you.

Signed,

Teddy Bear.

I rose from my seat and proceeded to the doorway.

Whoever wants to play this small thing with me. I'll tell you something about myself: I'm fascinated by mystery. Unfortunately, there was no Teddy Bear in this school, however, there was a performance called Army Of Teddy Bear in our last talent event. And the main role was a man dressed as a teddy bear named R. Edd Beaty, and the entire talent show was a fiasco since he had to move around by hopping in every scene. After all, because of the teddy bear outfit, both of his legs were joined, and it went wrong, especially in the final scene when he was supposed to jump away. Instead, he collided with someone who was carrying watermelon juice on a platter, and he was in shambles, and all the parents went home with his distinctive goodbye. So, I'm guessing that's why so many people spread rumours about him and he's at the top of the hatred list. I just think they should have practised instead of doing an unexpected event like talent shows usually do.

SEVEN

A "SECOND "RIDDLE & "ENCOUNTER" WITH EDD

After 5 seconds

Okay, that was a strange letter; I never imagined a nasty guy would strive to reveal his identity. If you haven't guessed who the bad guy is yet, let me tell you (R. Edd Beaty = Teddy Bear). Change the letters).

After a brief moment of reflection, I had an idea. Why don't I just play his game before busting him?

I got up and went to the back of the school, where I retrieved a piece of paper from the skip. I'm not sure how my eyes concentrated and caught that. In the mass of garbage was a blue piece of paper with a silver design that ended in 7 stripes. It stated,

I'm at the start of the Pain
and the end of Time

I'm sporty and fun
to play on
I conclude with big spacious halls
with a basketball court
5 cricket nets
and 2 badminton courts
I have a teacher who holds me
I am 2 words
Who am I?

When I noticed unexpected activity around me, I covered it, as if, nothing had happened. When I turned around, I expected to see myself alone in the back of the school, but instead, I saw myself looking at a boy (dressed in blue jeans, a white t-shirt, a brown denim jacket on top, and a black polyester silk bow tie).

"Looks like you just started the game," He said with a grin on his face

"You are Telly Belly"

"It's Teddy Bear"

"You're Ted?"

"No, I'm Edd"

"You're Dead, no! You're talking so I don't believe you"

"No, I'm Edd!"

"You're Bed?"

"No, I'm Edd!"

"You're Ned?"

"No, I'm Edd!"

"You're Fed, before lunch?"

"No, I'm Edd!"

"You're Edd"

"No, I'm Edd!"

"Are you sure"

"Huh"

"Anyway, yeah, I just happen to desperately want my friends back and also happen to be in a good mood, so I won't take revenge and will play your game for once."

"Amazing please don't cheat, if you do, just remember I'm holding your friends captive, HAAAA HAAAA HAAAA HAAAA HAAA HAA HA HA H_" And he made a bad man chuckle.

"Why are all evil people laughing so hard? Can't they chuckle or laugh like normal people?" I interrupted his E-Laugh.

And in an instant, he pulled a tiny sack from his pouch and tossed it to the ground.

The little sack puffed up, releasing what smelled like... chilli powder!!

I fled as fast as I could to keep the chilli powder out of my eyes by closing them tightly. Thankfully, the kitchen washroom was right ahead of me; unfortunately, a man with a cart full of rubbish to toss in the dumpsters, appeared from the kitchen's back door, and I smashed into it with full force, causing myself to fly through the wall and dive down onto the dumpster. When I got over the ache and stopped spinning my head like a fidget spinner. I dusted myself, washed my eyes, and then thought...

This is a simple puzzle.

The answer is...

P E

Phys Ed.

Class for Physical Education

EIGHT

A "PRELUDE" TO THE DOG'S COLLAR

5 minutes before lunch on Tuesday.

After the class was dismissed, I dashed to the Phys Ed class. The first thing I saw was a slew of electronic things on the table in the right corner of the room. Something caught my attention when I turned to the other side. I repeated the movement a few times to see if I could catch it again. But I couldn't do it.

After 5 seconds,

The nurse entered the room carrying a glass jar.

And she asked me in a gentle tone.

"What exactly are you looking for, Zach?"

"Nothing, there was some shimmering object I saw and was trying to find it, that's all,"

I said, trying not to appear suspicious, when a thought occurred to me.

"Okay, then," she answered, almost about to walk back when I asked...

"Miss..." I asked myself if she would turn around.

"I actually... came to ask you a question," almost hyperventilating now,

"Mmmhmm?" she responds eagerly.

"I heard that you made the dog's collar, so I wanted to ask you what it does?" feeling a blast of emotions, I ask. "What is it exactly?"

"That is some classified information, but I believe I can explain it to you..." she explains.

"Please do," I said, attempting to inquire about it.

"So... the Dog's collar is a small gas that I invented to help children heal (for 3-4 hours) when they get injuries. When I made the potion, I added too much green tea (which is used for releasing dopamine, which can help them mentally not stay depressed and heal faster, but too much dopamine can cause hallucinations and improper working of the body just like any drug you can find) for its smell, but then I added a bit too much of it that when people smelt it, instead of only getting cured, they also start hallucinating for 3-4 hours continuously, The adverse impact is that if they smell it for too long, their brain sorta' went idle and they obeyed whatever instruction was given to them by someone who isn't affected by it, which is why the school instructed everyone not to go near it."

"Is it what people call the dog flu when that happens?"

"Oh... no, no, no, no, no, no, the dog flu is just a rumour made up to keep children away from it."

"OK," I mumble under my breath, sighing.

"I hope you use this information wisely because your spy group may require it," she stated.

"Whaa... how did you_"

But before I knew it, she was gone. He winked as she moved her head just enough for me to view her left eye.

“O" my mouth is left making an 'O‘

Then suddenly, the shimmering thing drew my attention, and I spun around to see where it originated from. When I got closer, I noticed Faren’s jewellery, which her mother had given her for her birthday. She never went anywhere without it, so how did it end up here, I pondered, until I noticed a note next to it, which said...

You are known for being the most passive animal
When I dominate you, you are addicted to sugar.
If I'm sugar,
What exactly are you?

....

What exactly am I? I asked myself.

"A sugar zombie" I muttered

When I turned around I saw Edd again

Why does he keep coming whenever I find a clue

“Hi tedd”

“It’s Edd”

“Ok”

“Found a clue, huh”

“I’m playing the game ‘cause you have my team, that’s all so stop bugging me”

“I’m checking on you to make sure... you aren’t cheatin’”

“What d’ya’ want with the dog collar”

“Nunya’ business,” he said

“How many clues are left?”

“Nonnnnnnnn...... NONE!”

“You’re askin’ me to become a sugar zombie?”

“Kinda’, you’re strong and you know how to do business, so maybe”

“Offer dropped”

"Your friends are in grave danger!" "I'll make them walk the plank, Matey, you'll be swimming looking for them while they are in the tummy of sharks"

"I have my ways to do stuff and I know how you're just one of those who need attention, and when they have enough, they have power, and with the power, you'll gather everybody, and drop the bomb. And that's what you're planning for the Dog's collar, to have a group of Sugar Zombies that will listen to their master and do anything he asks, isn't it"

"Good job, you found my plan but the purpose is different"

"Kay then"

"I'll be waiting and also...... Bye!"

"Puuffff" another sack but this time it was white it was... flour

NINE

A "STOLEN" DARK GEM

Tuesday, 3:00 PM, after school.

I went to the cafeteria to discuss - my clue discoveries and encounter with Teddy Bear - with my buddies. I was so caught up in my mind with this case that I had forgotten about the "Dream Valentine's Dance" aka DVD, which was set to be happening "THIS FRIDAY."

Our school (Dream Point) celebrated Valentine's Day two days earlier than usual because the school's anniversary was two days earlier than Valentine's Day, therefore earning the name "Dream Valentines Dance." (This time it was on a Friday, and The Spy Team offered to help engineer and make props.)

I was expected to meet everyone in the cafeteria after school to assist in the creation of props such as chocolate fountains, strawberry cakes, disco lights, entrance, plants, nutritious food, snacks, laptops, banners, DJ settings, arcade games, stage decorations, wi-fi, sanitisers, and the best of all - **"The Dark Gem's Display"**

Anyway, as I walked into the cafeteria, everyone ignored me, and I had no idea what they were doing until... Faren and Jayden raised a big banner that said...

The Dream Valentines Dance

Friday at 6 p.m. Please attend!!!

And then a slew of disco lights appeared on the ground, accompanied by music.

I glanced towards the music, Kelly was DJing, the chocolate fountain was flowing, the arcade games were on, and everything was going as planned. It was incredible, That's when I recalled I needed to grab the rainbow-coloured doorway I constructed at home, complete with arcade drawings, doodle chocolate, and the "Dark Gem's display." The Dark Gem was a diamond with dark magic power, thus the name, and anyone who received it would get the abilities that are received by users of Dark Magic, thus you would need to grasp it with rubber gloves to avoid getting the power (similar to electricity it also has an insulator). The diamond was discovered by Principal Tom's Great-Great-Great-Grandfather and passed down through generations to him; every 10th anniversary of the school, he placed it in a large glass dome; this year, the 75th anniversary of the school since its construction, he wanted to showcase it since it was three-fourths of a century since the school was built.

Because it was the 75th anniversary, it was extra special. I dashed to the chamber where I stored the entryway and the dome without the Dark Gem, unlocked the door, and rolled the entryway and dome to the cafeteria because they were on a tiny platform with wheels. When I came to the door, everyone was surprised, perhaps because I did an excellent job on my project and it appeared that I hadn't worked on anything at all due to the case. That's when Principal Tom stormed in from the rear of the cafeteria, clutching a piece of paper. He glanced around and discovered me at the front door of the cafeteria.

He dashed up to me and cried...

"The Gem has vanished!" "Someone took it."

"Which gem?" I said, my voice full of interest.

"Whoever stole the Dark Gem is in grave danger. If not, we are."

I was taken aback, and then I perceived who it was...

Are you thinking about what I'm thinking (you, the reader)... you know what I mean. Edddddd!! So that was his strategy. How could we have forgotten?

TEN

A "CLASH" WITH THE "THREE MUSKETEERS"

Thursday, 6:00 a.m., before Physical Education.

We investigated yesterday and discovered nothing. We went throughout the school and tried all we could to find it, but we found nothing, nothing, nothing, nothing, and nothing. We were ready to give up the case, and I was poised to be the most boring leader in the history of boring/lamest leaders, winning the Award of boring/lamest leaders, when something mega, something oblivious, something mind-blowing, something terrifying, something scary happened.

Our system gates that led to the hidden club in the centre of the school began to display something we hadn't seen in 5 years (that's what they said).

"It's happening again, people," someone remarked.

"Someone hacked into our systems. Guys, go shut everything down and evacuate!" Said Jake (indeed, Fariq's folks knew he was a spy in their clan and hence Kicked him out).

It's never happened to me before.

We rushed to the escape portals, but the portals were broken for some reason. The rest of them activated the slides which led outside of the school I was left with no option other than being trapped. I tried hitting the emergency button since it activates a large slide that leads to the outside of the school, and it worked. I slipped and slid and slid till we came to a halt. Someone anticipated our evacuation and blocked the slides and the emergency slide with paper mache that smelled like chilli powder... Oh, noooooo!!!!!

Are you wondering why I despise chilli powder? Because I am allergic to it, if I smell it, I will sneeze profusely and may get rashes. I was ready to quit when I realised...

I have sticky shoe mode on my shoes and sticky gloves in my pockets (yeah, I have a bestie named Kristi who makes all of these cool gadgets, and sticky shoes and gloves were his latest inventions, and in my shoe, he has drill mode, skate mode, bounce mode, freeze mode, oil slick mode, and all kinds of cool stuff.)

I utilised my sticky shoes and gloves to get to where I slid, then I grabbed a grappling hook and threw it into another of my classmate's slides, and I shouted.

I summoned the bravery to look down the slide when I saw the hole was empty, then I glanced at my hole, which was still blocked, and then I looked at all the holes except my own, which were all open, so I went down by one of them. When I heard people chatting, I slowed down in my boots to avoid alerting anyone and hid behind a bush. I saw Ed talking to Fariq, and the youngster I saw yesterday when I looked at him clearly through a leaf of the bush, I saw that he was wearing a nametag of wood with the name R.

Robin Beaty carved on it, Then I noticed something else on Ed's leather jacket with the same sort of name tag but with the name, R. Edd Beaty, and I believed I saw another one elsewhere... I couldn't remember who it was, but I knew I had seen it somewhere. At that time, they began sharing their plan for what to do with the Dark Gem, and I began recording it all with my recording tie, where I had a camera and an audio recorder, and they were saying things like this...

"We should wait until 6:30 when everyone goes to get a snack, and then let the fume out," Edd said.

"And I'll divert the attention of all the spies and that little ignorant leader of theirs."Said Fariq equally disgusted as I was.

"I will inform the teachers that they must all go to the storage room to retrieve a large chocolate fountain and that they must all go because it is heavy and one person cannot do it alone." So after they're all gone, I'll lock the door behind them," Robin explained.

"Then I'll go to the principal's cabin and tell him we found the dark gem in the boy's bathroom, and when he goes there, we'll lock that door as well, and then we'll go and take the red stone from the shelf and behind the book, Nature gives you a wonderful life," Edd stated

"When that happens we will ask everybody to go to the science classroom for a movie since there is a big projector over there when they enter we shall release the fume and we shall conquer the world, though I don't know what we will do after that," said Robin

"Well, before that we ne_" I had moved because all that staying still made me itch in my foot, and I did a small itch that's when a twig under my foot snapped. The attention was on me, again like on the rooftop of the school, and with all my might and courage - I ran! For My Life. That's when I saw my whole team tied up to a tree with a rope and guarding them were some dozen bodyguards. I also happened to see the guy who I just remembered had the same wooden badge on his chest Fariq, Fariq Bates my AEF. That's when Robin shouted,

"GET HIM!!!!!"

I ran as fast as anything thankfully luck was on my side today and the bell rang, and I joined the sea of students pushing their way through to the classrooms on the opposite side of the school I had never run so fast in my life I must have been faster than the fastest man on earth. Damn! the three musketeers. They are really up to no good.

ELEVEN

A "BULL-Y CHASE"

Physical Education, 7:00 a.m.

I became increasingly stressed about people spying on me, and I couldn't concentrate on one of my favourite training sessions.

The coach summoned me to his desk on the right side of the entryway after five minutes. I dashed up to him, hoping he wouldn't notice anything was wrong with me. He then informed me that my football kicks, frisbee throws, rope and rock climbing attempts had all dropped today. Then he asked me,

"What's the matter with you, Zach?" Why do you seem a little odd, perhaps more off than the day your tooth went loose?

"Uhh" I stuttered

"No Uhhs. tell me whatever is wrong."He pushes me to get to the point.

"Nothing, it's just that I'm afraid something bad might happen on the DVD." And I'm taking up all the tension and trying to fix it. I explain,

"Leave that to the teachers." Now is the time to have fun rather than complain about something. If you're not paying attention to your body, you may have a sprained ankle or whatever." He stated.

"It also shouldn't be about the chocolate fountain." I've heard that white chocolate is available every 10 minutes. It's going to be delectable!" He yelled.

And he extended his arms and pointed to the people working out, motioning for me to join them.

8: 30 a.m., after Physical Education

I dashed to my locker and pulled on my hoodie so no one could see my face.

I continued strolling to the cafeteria, where I drank a packet of orange juice and ate a chocolate and blueberry pie energy bar. As I approached the dining, an announcement over the speakers said something like.

"All of the hall monitors join Fariq's bodyguards to apprehend Zach Quinn." He has taken Fariq's golden watch; please watch for him and, again, apprehend Zach Quinn for stealing our president's golden wristwatch."

I rushed towards the storage room on the left hallway of the lobby because no one used it anymore except for some students who used the dumbwaiter in there to move to other levels, or so I thought.

When I looked in I saw something stunning they all had hundreds of treats and chocolates and candies in them they were like a big stock of them. That's when a puzzle clicked in my head - *The sugar zombies I saw were getting the sweets and treats from here.*

So I started taking pictures of all the enormous boxes that were placed in front of some people guarding and walking around the place. I noticed those folks collecting handfuls of chocolates, bubblegums and other delicacies and placing them in box after box, that of which they grabbed and placed in the old dumbwaiter we used to use,

And this time another puzzle clicked in my head - *the dumbwaiters were closed down 3 days ago because it broke down in the middle of taking some luggage to the 3rd floor so they said that it needs repair and they closed it the broken down dumbwaiter looks like,* this was probably just an excuse for being able to do this. Then I for some felt that Principal Tom had something to do with this because he was the one who asked me for details on the team who led "**The Sugar Zombies**".

TWELVE

A "HERO" WHO WORE THE "FIREBALL 2879"

I also happened to have a tie that Kristi gave me, He said the Tie records and uploads videos to The Spy Teams Cloud and the whole school can watch things from there (both live and pre-recorded). He also mentioned how the Tie reflects light easily in fact it gives so much light in the darkness even the moon cannot match it.

I then carefully placed my tie on top of a crate at that time, until a guy started approaching me.

RUN!

I turned off the audio and camera, took off the tie, and ran, while letting it upload to the cloud and then I chucked it away trying to create a diversion. I ran through the boxes until I hit a very heavy one and tumbled close to the lift. When my eyes adjusted to the darkness; I got up and saw Anthony, the school's best football player, with his gang of bullies.

He dashed after me, holding duct tape in his hand. I sprinted over boxes and jumped over them to the entrance on the other side of the room, and when I reached there, I snatched a box and flung it behind me, causing one of Anthony's men to collapse. Then I grabbed another and tossed it back, and another of Anthony's thugs collapsed. I hurried out the door, motioning for everyone to move out of the path. I dashed to the cafeteria to inform the principal of what had occurred wh_, Yeah, that's where I started the story, but after that, I went to the corner of the cafeteria and was about to cry when someone grabbed me and pulled me down to a table close to me, and I was about to cry out saying don't kill me. Until I saw it was Kristi who pulled me down.

"It's me, take off your suit and right foot shoe and put on this," he stated, pointing to a large robot shoe.

"What exactly does it do?" I muttered

"Just put it on! If you want to live" I removed my shoe and black coat and wore only the shoe.

That's when I started becoming bigger and bigger until I was in a robot (that was the size of Anthony) heading towards the principal when the robot asked me a question.

"Where exactly do you want to go?"

"Go ahead, ummm... "2879 Fireball" I read it on the shoe's side.

"That's fine, you can call me Ay-ven-ine." Replied the robot

I walked to Principal Tom and the whole story flowed out of my mouth, and then I talked about how they captured the whole of BCHQ and how we hadn't done anything about the sweet stalls that were held on the rooftop, and then I finally connected everything on how Fariq, Edd, and Robin planned what they were going to do for DVD and how they stole **The Dark Gem.**

I didn't see Principal Tom depart or the hall monitors enter throughout all of the excitement. When I saw them, I hid behind a curtain and made myself back to how I was by pushing a button on the shoe I put the shoe in my bag and walked towards them surrendering, but then something strange happened they said thanks to me for leading them to the sugar zombies and left, I asked them if they knew about Fariq's, Edd's, and Robin's plans they said they didn't have too much proof and I showed them the cloud and they thanked me and went thankfully. But I had one last task: **Apologise. To. My. Friends.**

Okay, so I lied. I apologise.

I stood up and walked to my locker. When Jayden, Faren, Kelly, and Jake approached me,

"I... I'm so_" I was going to say anything when Kelly cut me off.

"We are the ones who should be sorry."

"Yeah, we were kind of selfish and never stuck by your side." Jayden elaborated

"How did you manage to escape?" I inquired, hoping to lighten the atmosphere. Kristi appeared at the same time.

"I gave Kelly a headphone with spikes, and she cut the rope with that," he explained.

"Sweet," I rolled my eyes.

"Who's planning on going to the dance tomorrow?" Jayden stated

"I am," I stated.

Oh, yes. I nearly forgot about the three musketeers (Edd, Robin, and Fariq) They were suspended for a week, then detained after school for two weeks, and Edd's and Robin's clan, as well as the booths on the rooftop, were demolished and broken down, while Fariq got stripped of his role as student president and his bodyguards were taken away until the next student council elections. Because I am the hero. (as well as my dependable companions)

THIRTEEN

CONCLUSION

Friday, The DVD

Being the wonderful boy I am, I went to the DVD. It was wonderful. Sitting under the night sky eating strawberries with chocolate, having cakes, and chips, while others in my group had partners and were dancing. you might think I was sad alone or something but I am used to (and love) being with myself and reflecting on the week after all it was Adventure-Packed. My taste for an adventure this week has grown old. It needed some relaxation and comfort, it needed a sense of.........Happiness and JOY. And I got what I needed and to sprinkle a bit of happiness all my friends came together to have fun.

Today was a fun and exciting day. This entire week was exciting and exciting. This was the most enjoyable experience I've ever had, and I intend to capture it. Hopefully, when I become famous, my story will be a huge success, and a million people all over the world will read it. Today is the day I began my journey, hand in hand with my desire to be a spy. Maybe I'll start a business or become renowned. But, whatever the possibilities are, I'll be there with my spy team.

Looking back at myself and what I accomplished, I am shocked that I am not renowned or remembered as the youngster who experienced the biggest catastrophe in his life. My reality is much like yours, but what distinguishes it is...my Purpose. Everyone, from an ant to a person, has a particular purpose. Every person in this world serves a purpose in some way. And my way to achieve my purpose (to make a change in this world) is to be a spy!!

THE END

www.ingramcontent.com/pod-product-compliance
Lightning Source LLC
La Vergne TN
LVHW091234150826
845673LV00003B/1135